In the beginning there was . . .

ink.

FROM

Death

Comes a Scribbler

A TRIBUTE TO THE MASTER EDWARD GOREY

Sibling
Press

CONTENTS

April 17th, 2000

I dreamed I saw Edward Gorey last night. He came and said to me...

"Although you have heard otherwise, I am not dead, you see."

"I float among the clouds at night ...

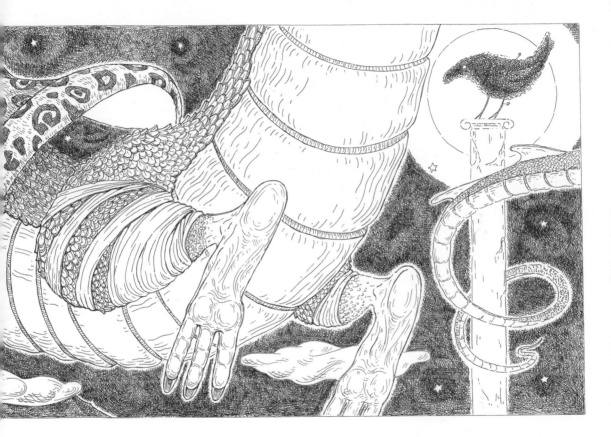

and into dreams," said he.

"But Ed," I said, "You're two days dead."

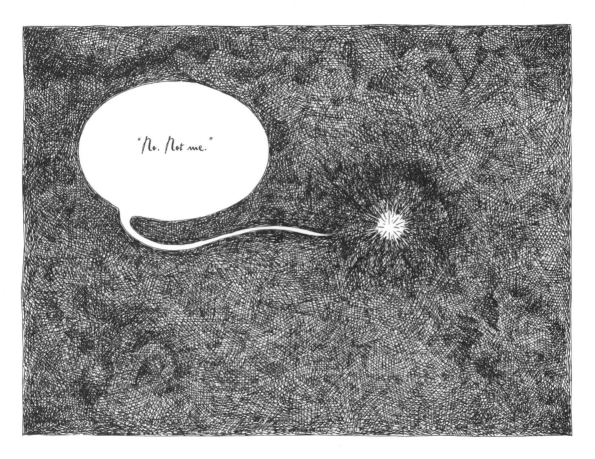

"No," said Ed, "Not me."

My thoughts, I weave into you now, and laugh and dance with glee.

For now that I am up above, I glide and sway with ease."

LITERARY
KNO~

~arison Human Nature Foresig~

Intuition

Criticis~

"Now Ed," I said,
"You're in my head,
what do I do with Thee?"

My friend...until the end...

...until you're dead like me.

Well...,thank you sir. It sounds absurd.
But yes, I will abide.

"FOR YOU!,"

I said, "My dear friend Ed.

FOR YOU,

I will contrive."

You must be...

I dreamed I saw Edward Gorey last night.

He came and said to me,

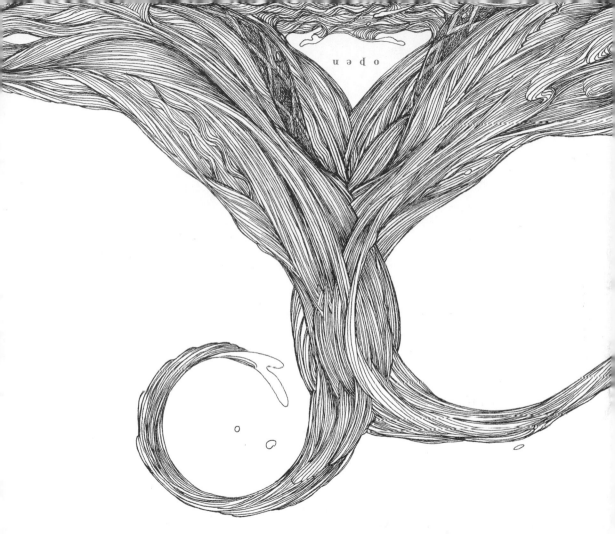

open

o p e n

"Although you may think otherwise,
I am not dead you'll see."

THE END

EDWORDS

EDWARD ST. JOHN GOREY died on April 15th, 2000, leaving behind fans who

will feel his absence and his presence through his one hundred and thirty witty and

spirited books. As an animal lover, the Humane Society was one of

his many shelters of choice, as well as animal welfare in general.

For your further enjoyment, visit www.goreyhouse.org.

Edward Gorey Bibliography

Edward Gorey Bibliography

Deadicated to Mikey

MY CAT WHO, SAW ME THROUGH THIS BOOK
AND THEN, HIMSELF, EXPIRED.

V.S.

SIBLING PRESS WISHES TO THANK ALL OF OUR FAMILY AND FRIENDS FOR THE SUPPORT AND

ENCOURAGEMENT TO PURSUE DREAMS THAT WILL JUST NOT GO AWAY.

THE UNKNOWN SCRIBBLER WISHES TO THANK: ROBERT ROSENWALD AND POISONED PEN PRESS FOR THE CHANCE, MICHAEL KAHN, FOR HIS

GUIDANCE, JUANITA HAVILL FOR HER GOOD NATURE AND OTHER PROFESSIONAL SKILLS, JASON O'LEARY FOR HIS EXPERTISE, AND TO

AVA, SCOTT AND DAVID FOR KEEPING HER GROUNDED. ALSO TO HER CHRONIC GOD AND TO HER IMMORTAL BELOVED.

PRINTED IN CHINA

FIRST EDITION

ISBN 0-9654265-1-3

IN PREPARATION BY

The Unknown Scribbler

PONDERING MARY

THE GAINING

MY LEFT BREAST

LITTLE DIDACTIC WE

THE WICKED DAUGHTER

YOUR SISTER IS NOT KINDLING

BATS, BONES AND ICKY SMELLS

BEETHOVEN'S HAIR

THE POSSIBLE FABLE

THE PEDESTRIAN POET

SURROGATE THOUGHTS

THE BEWILDERING FACT

MY CHRONIC GOD

WWW.SIBLINGPRESS.COM

Sibling Press, the home of The Unknown Scribbler, is devoted to offering dribbles of thought and obsessive observations in pen from the reluctant artist/poet. With influences from pen and ink artists such as Beardsley, Sime, Goya, Lear, Clark, and of course, Edward Gorey, The Unknown Scribbler feels it a humbling honor and pleasure to offer ink to paper to viewer.

Former maid, bartender and waitress, The Unknown Scribbler, in another life, has also been an editorial illustrator, book, and graphic designer for over 20 years. Her work appeared in the Los Angeles Times Book Review section for over a decade and continues to have editorial illustrations syndicated nationally. Also as a mother and wife, The Unknown Scribbler has her share of sleep deprivation and clutter. She would not have it any other way.

Our goal at Sibling Press is to offer a donation to a charitable cause that is linked to, or inspired by a book's subject.